The Bravest Knight
Who Ever Lived

Written by Daniel Errico

Illustrated by Shiloh Penfield

Schiffer Publishing Ltd

4880 Lower Valley Road • Atglen, PA 19310

The Bravest Knight
Who Ever Lived

Other Schiffer Books on Related Subjects:

Unraveling Rose by Brian Wray, illustrated by Shiloh Penfield, ISBN: 978-0-7643-5393-2

Edited by Jesse Marth
Type set in Altenglisch/A780 Deco/Scrivano
Designed by Jack Chappell
ISBN: 978-0-7643-5690-2
Printed in China

Co-published by Pixel Mouse House &
Schiffer Publishing, Ltd.
4880 Lower Valley Road
Atglen, PA 19310
Phone: (610) 593-1777; Fax: (610) 593-2002
E-mail: Info@schifferbooks.com
Web: www.schifferbooks.com

For our complete selection of fine books on this and related subjects, please visit our website at www.schifferbooks.com. You may also write for a free catalog.

Schiffer Publishing's titles are available at special discounts for bulk purchases for sales promotions or premiums. Special editions, including personalized covers, corporate imprints, and excerpts, can be created in large quantities for special needs. For more information, contact the publisher.

We are always looking for people to write books on new and related subjects. If you have an idea for a book, please contact us at proposals@schifferbooks.com.

This Book Belongs To:

To Your Story.

Once upon a time, inside a kingdom like your own,
There lived a knight named Cedric, the bravest ever known.

He grew up poor and honest, on a humble pumpkin farm.
He treated people well and kind and never did them harm.

For breakfast, he had pumpkins, and for dinner, pumpkin stew.
I'd like to say dessert was not, but it was pumpkin too.

He liked to play pretend and all his friends would join, too.
They met inside a wooden castle, plotting what to do.

Before they started playing, he would dress for every quest,
Pumpkin armor on his head, on his arms, and on his chest.

He battled trolls and dragons. He defeated many foes.
Afterwards, a princess offered him a single rose.

"Cedric, you have saved her!" cheered his most excited friends.
But always he would just reply, "That isn't how it ends."

One day, he went out scouting, hiding high upon a tree,
Looking for a day to save, as far as he could see.

A fancy carriage rolled up slowly, stopping just below.
The driver wasn't certain which direction he should go.

Suddenly a thief approached, disguised with cloak and hood.
Cedric knew the bandit wasn't up to any good.

The driver ran away and left the carriage to the thief.
Cedric peered from up above, behind an autumn leaf.

"Stop right there!" he shouted as he tossed an acorn shell.
It landed on the carriage roof and rang it like a bell.

"Who's there??" replied the bandit, as he peeked outside to see,
"A dozen royal archers," Cedric answered from the tree.

As Cedric shook the branches, fifty acorns tumbled down.
The bandit fled the carriage, to the woods away from town.

The knight who owned the carriage gave his thanks when it returned.
He offered to young Cedric all the lessons he had learned.

"To be a knight," he lectured Cedric, "takes a special sort.
It isn't always jousting and attending royal court."

"You must protect the weak. Be always true, be always strong.
And more than any other, you must see the right from wrong."

"But," Cedric protested, "I am just a pumpkin farmer."
"Now you are a squire," said the knight, "now go get my armor!"

For years the knight taught Cedric how to battle, how to ride.

Wherever he would go, his squire followed by his side.

And then one day the knight retired, hanging up his steel.
He brought his squire out to court and asked that he would kneel.

"I dub you now 'Sir Cedric.' You're a true and worthy knight.
You've courage in your bones," he said, "now go and prove me right!"

So, off he set to find his path with nothing but his horse.

Well . . . he also packed a piece of peppered pumpkin pie, of course.

Somewhere on the road, between the here, before the there,
He came upon a blackened castle, desolate and bare.

The sign read "Dragon Castle, All You Hero Knights Beware!
Fiery Dragon Breath Awaits, Continue If You Dare!"

He took his armor off, so he could swim the murky moat.
"Just my luck," he mumbled, "I forgot to pack a boat!"

In the yard, he noticed rows of pumpkins in a patch.
His family's weren't as large, but they were otherwise a match.

He donned his pumpkin armor as he'd done when he was young.
Often, we can find the answers back where we've begun.

Then suddenly Sir Cedric heard a loud, tremendous roar.
A dragon flew right for him, crashing through the tower door!

She breathed her fiery breath and Cedric thought that he was toasted.
But Cedric had been saved; instead his armor had been roasted!

He threw it off and soon the dragon ate it like a feast.
"Roasted pumpkin," Cedric yelled, "a favorite of the beast!"

As the dragon chewed, Sir Cedric gathered pumpkin shells.
He filled them up with water from the dragon castle wells.

The dragon wasn't finished. She was hungry for some more.
Cedric threw her pumpkins by the two, then by the four.

Cedric had a plan the munching dragon did not know.
For in the dragon's stomach, a small pool began to grow.

So, when she turned to Cedric with a fire-breathing shout,
She found that all the fire in her belly had gone out!

A prince and princess ran outside to thank their fearless knight.
"That dragon took us," said the prince, "but now we'll be all right!"

Cedric and the siblings made the lengthy journey back.
The prince and Cedric walked along and shared a pumpkin snack.

They talked about their homes and of their favorite games to play.
The two of them grew close along the long and windy way.

The queen and king came out and gave their children royal hugs.

They gave Sir Cedric gold, and silk, and much-too-fancy rugs.

Cedric just refused, no matter how they tried and tried.
But then the princess said that she would like to be his bride.

"Princess, you are kind, and I am glad that we are friends.
But now I must be brave and say that isn't how it ends."

"There's someone else I love, and I believe we're meant to be.
I'd like to wed the prince if he does feel the same for me."

The prince was overjoyed, and yet, the king, a bit confused.
At first he didn't understand. At first he had refused.

But as he saw their faces, in his heart the truth was clear.
His son was meant to find his knight. He needn't doubt or fear.

They threw a royal wedding, like you've never seen before.
Pumpkins, trumpets, rows of cakes, and doves were set to soar.

And Cedric took a breath and told himself he'd be all right.
For everyone gets nervous, even he, the bravest knight.

A celebration roared with all their family and their friends,
And Cedric knew, "My fairy tale . . . this is how it ends."

A Message from the United Nations Human Rights Office

The world is made up of all kinds of people. More than seven and a half billion people of all shapes and sizes, each with their own hopes and dreams, wants and worries.

While we all might be different from one another, we're all born equal. No one is any more or less valuable than anyone else.

That's why everyone has the same "human rights." Human rights are things we should all have, or be able to do – no matter who we are, or where we come from.

No one should be punished for being themselves. No one should be treated unfairly because of whom they love.

The United Nations is working to make sure that no children or young people are bullied because of who they are or whom they love. You can find out more here: www.unfe.org/end-bullying.

We can all do our part to treat those around us with respect and friendship. Because while it's okay to be different, it's not okay to be treated unfairly just because you are.

And they lived happily ever after . . .